In My Dreams

Underlayes, Volume 3

T. A. Moorman

Published by GothicMom's Studios, 2020.

IN MY DREAMS

First edition. May 10, 2020.

ISBN: 978-1393533566

Written by T. A. Moorman.

Also by T. A. Moorman

Underlayes
Witch Wars
Hybrids
The Succubus, The Demon, and The Witch
In My Dreams
Chocolate Vanilla Swirl

Standalone
Santa's Curse
Wait, You Did What?
Allergic Reaction
Not So Wicked
Lady Killers

Watch for more at gothicmoms.blogspot.com.

Abuse can come in many ways, shapes, and forms, and no one deserves to go through it. Someone told me that if you love someone you can take their abuse. That isn't true. If that person truly loves you, they wouldn't want you to suffer any abuse, especially from them.

Underlayes

Underlayes is another dimension, where all sorts of nocturnal creatures reside: witches, vampires, fae, shifters, werewolves... The dimension was created by all these creatures working side by side to escape the scrutiny and danger to their very existence that stemmed from the human world. Humans tend to fear things they do not understand, and tend to try to eliminate anything they fear, even though these nocturnal beings were humanoid themselves, just different—more enhanced—than their day-walking brethren.

When God created the Earth, He had some help along the way. While there is only one true God, there are many underling goddesses and gods to help Him. Let's just think of God as the CEO. Just as God created man in His image, He allowed His goddesses and gods to create certain races in their images as well. Their races come in every color, shape and form there is, but are like them in their... characteristics. Like, for instance, Hekate and her necromancers, or Aphrodite and her beautiful sirens. Since most of these creatures are more powerful when the moon comes out to play, they are nocturnal, though don't get it wrong; they are not ruled by the moon. Some have a deadly reaction to the sun, while others are just as powerful be it day or night.

Many of these creatures can be quite deadly, though it's usually only when provoked. Though there are some who tend to be more violent and sadistic, regular humans can be that way as well. After all, most serial killers, though not all, are human.

Originally the intention was for these nocturnal creatures to have their time at night and keep to themselves, while regular humans were to rule the day, unawares. Most had perfected their art of blending in whenever the need arose, since there was no way to live in the same realm as humans and not bump into one, whether on purpose or by folly. Certain precautions were made and set into place for when any of these other species came into contact with a human. Necessary precautions were also in place to deal the elements; such as the sun and the moon.

Prologue

I don't know why so many people always wish they had a do over in life. I mean, I guess I get it in a way. And probably more-so would if what happened to me hadn't happened. But it did.

I have no memory of the life I led before being turned. Ricardo, my Fated One, and I had been together for only a year, but it felt like I knew him for much longer than that. He said that memory loss was something that sometimes happened to the newly turned. I took his word for it, since that's not exactly something you can just look up on Google without finding a bunch of nonsense. And we stayed in a pretty tight-lipped community, amongst others like us. But no one delved into anyone else's business. There were some we were friendly with, but not really friends. He said the night he turned me I had been on the brink of death, that he had found me in an alley left for dead. That he knew me before in passing, and couldn't just let me die. We've been together ever since.

I woke up after having yet another dream that felt like much more than just that, with my entire body feeling as if I had just done an entire triatholon the night before. I sat up and put my head in my hands, my head feeling like it was in a vice grip from hell. It had been happening for the past few weeks, and had been getting worse instead of better.

I climbed out of bed, careful to not wake Ricardo. It was early still, but I had no intentions of going back to sleep, no way was I risking having another one of those dreams. They hurt too much to wake up from. They weren't nightmares, far from it, but when I woke up they were fragments I couldn't manage to piece together. But for some reason I almost always found myself if not in pain, then in tears when I woke up from them. And not just that, there was some form of power inside of me trying to break free, but I had no idea what it was or how to access it, yet.

Stepping into the bathroom I didn't bother with turning on the light, just slipped my black lace chemise over my head and stepped into our large, walk-in shower, and turned the water as hot as I could bare it. As I stood there directly under the spray flashes of a man kept appearing behind my eyelids. I could barely make out his features, but for whatever reason not being able to recognize him made me more than just sad, but hollow inside like something was missing.

"Rena, why are you up so early love? The sun has just barely set." As quiet as I had been getting out of the bed I must have still woken Ricardo. I was so lost in thought that I hadn't even heard him open the shower door. He stood directly behind me and pulled my body flush against his own, swept my hair to the side and gently grazed his fangs along the crook of my neck before letting them sink into my skin.

Ricardo was not a male of many words, but what he lacked in syllables he made up for in sensation. His cold body grew warmer as he fed from me, I could feel his shaft growing and hardening against the crease of my ass. The water cascaded down both of our bodies as he licked the bite marks closed, and his large hands began to work their magic. With one hand, he began kneading my breast, squeezing right to the borderline between pleasure and pain as his other slid down to my hips then around my waist until it found the shaved, heated entrance that was waiting for him. He slipped his fingers, not inside of me, but only slid them along my tight, wet folds, then to tweak and tug at my clitoris, the sensation of that alone enough to put me on the verge of climax.

I whimpered as he removed his hand, but he was by no means done with me yet. Ricardo bent me slightly, splaying his pale ivory hand over my own, much smaller mocha one, interlacing our fingers along the tiles of the shower as I grabbed onto it for purchase. He then entered me in one swift, hard stroke. I screamed out as the feel of his long, wide shaft filled me so completely that if he wasn't an expert at using it, it would have hurt, instead it felt so good that my juices were already flowing around him. I came again as he found that perfect rhythm, his heavy length sliding up against my walls, the sensation making me so dizzy I would have lost my grip on the wall had he not still had hold of my hand. The water from the showerhead only added to the sensations.

Just as I felt myself coming to a full-on climax, the lightning bolt shaped mark on my outer thigh began to burn. The pain of it made me bend over further, making him not only go deeper, but also made me tighten even further around him. I became a mixture of both pleasure and true pain all at once, I could barely recognize which of the two my moans reflected. Ricardo slid out of me then, and before I had a chance to feel the emptiness of his shaft no longer there, he had me turned around, lifted up with a crushing grip on my hips, and was impaling me once again. As though he felt a sense of urgency, he pistoned in and out of me even harder and faster than before, which took my mind away from the flaring pain in my thigh.

As Ricardo gave me another stroke so deep inside of me I felt his sac rubbing against my entrance I screamed out with one last climax as he jettisoned inside, the warm trickling feel of it making me come that much harder. But when I closed my eyes, I was looking into the metallic silver irises that haunted my dreams, and they looked angry as hell. I could almost hear a faint, foreign, yet familiar voice in the back of my mind saying, *I will find you.*

When I opened my eyes, Ricardo was staring straight into mine, but it felt like he was seeing right through me to somewhere else, especially when he said, "She's mine."

Before I could ask him anything or think any further, he claimed my lips in a claiming, almost punishing kiss. Then I felt a tiny pinprick on the side of my hip and promptly blacked out.

***

Halfway across the world from where Ricardo and Rena were, a warlock wearing only a pair of black shorts, knelt down on the ground in the rain in the dark of night in a cemetery, the droplets shimmered down his muscled, ebony chest and back. He summoned the lightning to the palms of his outstretched hands, letting it empower him further, as he called out to his ancestors. "Ancestors, my foremothers, and forefathers, I come to you tonight, the anniversary of the night you gifted me with one of my greatest gifts, to ask your help in finding her. Help me bring her back to where she belongs, at my side."

The storm became malevolent then, lightning struck around Jonathan left and right, which both fueled and empowered him. He threw his head back as he soaked it all in. As he closed his eyes, his haunches rose when he finally saw her, with the vampire that had somehow ensnared his powerful, beautiful mate. He tried yet again to communicate with her through their mark, but something was blocking him still, but he felt it slipping, and that little slip was all he needed to learn her location.

Reaching into his back pocket, Jonathan pulled out his phone and dialed his brother. Without bothering with any pleasantries, all he said was, "It's time to hunt us down a vampire, and bring home my mate."

Chapter 1

"Spill the beans woman before I lose my ever-loving mind." I loved making Kenya wait, she was the most impatient female I knew. Lizzie was turning beat red as she did her best not to laugh. Whether from the expressions on Kenya's face, or the bright pink lipstick she'd decided to try that seemed to glow I had no idea. Maybe it was both. Kenya sat back in her seat and crossed her arms at her very ample chest, which drew more attention to the blindingly bright yellow dress she had on. The way she was dressed was a sure sign the two of them must have had a fight about something. It was the only time Kenya pulled out the tackiest looking clothes she could find. And with her exotic midnight sky complexion the neon bright material looked like it was actually glowing in the dark, and it was broad daylight.

"Lizzie, did you really have to piss her off today?" I eyeballed her as I asked the question and did my best to hold in the laugh bubbled up in my throat. Lizzie looked conservative in comparison to her mate. She wore a black leather catsuit which only had one sleeve, the other didn't have so much as a spaghetti strap which showed off her slightly muscular milky cream arm. With her blonde hair pulled to the top of her head in a sleek ponytail and cut bangs that hung right below her eyebrows she looked like she had just walked off the Charlies Angels film set. The two of them already resembled night and day as it was, without Kenya's added antics. "I mean, come on. How am I supposed to give y'all all the details you've been waiting to hear while trying to avoid looking at a Rainbow Brite reject for too long? Is she doing an experiment that neither of us know about? Can supes go blind, and if so what kind?"

Lizzie couldn't stop the laugh that came from her mouth, which was unfortunate considering she had just taken a huge sip of her extra red bubbly. Good thing she had on black. One of the waiters came rushing over with more than a few extra napkins as Lizzie began to explain, "Your friend has a case of baby fever and is doing her level best to pass it on to me." Was her sultry reply.

"So?" That really didn't explain much, not given their situation, "Lizzie, I thought the two of you worked that out a long time ago. That you were going to start your family right around now. It's been, what, twenty-five years now, right?" That earned me a scoff and an eyeroll from Kenya.

Lizzie went on to say to me, "Having the baby isn't what the problem is. The problem is that she wants me to be the one to carry it. That was *not* part of the deal, and she knows it."

"But you handle pain so much better than I do." Kenya replied as she did her level best to pout with her arms crossed against her chest. Which only made Lizzie and I laugh that much harder.

Once I was finally able to curtail my laughter I asked Kenya, "So you mean to tell me you over there huffin and puffin over something you have no business being mad about?" when she made no attempt to respond I continued, "Why would you even want Lizzie to carry the baby? She's part of the Guard you whacko." I laughed a bit more when she rolled her eyes at that, "Goddess, I really missed this."

"You're the one that decided to take a ten-year honeymoon." Lizzie said as she scooted back her chair and stood, "Now, if you'll excuse me, I think I see my dinner. Don't spill any details until I get back."

After she bent down to give Kenya a kiss on her still pouting, bright lips, Lizzie sashayed off to the dancefloor where willing donors were dancing to some new techno beat. We were at Club Vamptasy. That had been my first visit since it had been built while I was still abroad on my honeymoon. Apparently, the royal families created a new bar or club in each district as peace offerings after the wars. Well, they called them the wars, but if you asked me it was more like a huge family feud between the vampires, witches, and Rasputins, with a few others caught in the crossfire. Guess it was just one of those 'all in how you look at it' things. The clubs weren't segregated or anything stupid such as that, just each catered to specific factions needs. But everyone was allowed to come and have a good time.

At Club Vamptasy, the snack bar was literally on the dance floor. Human donors of every variety swayed to the beat with their necks and wrists exposed. If a vampire wanted to take a more intimate vein they had to do so in one of the private rooms in the back. I hadn't been to a private room or the snack bar yet, didn't have a need. I had already fully fed before I left home. To each their own and all that, but I'd much rather feed at home than in public. Guess a part of me would just always be a tad bit shy. Though my mate did tend to bring out my wild side; which is part of the reason I left him at home. The other part was that he was out catching up with his own friends.

I don't think I could have stopped smiling had I wanted to as I my eyes locked onto Kenya as she watched her wife sink her fangs into one of the women on the dance floor, "My Goddess, does the euphoric feeling ever go away?" I absently asked her.

"No." Kenya laughed slightly before she continued, her eyes still glued to the female she loved, "Do not get me wrong, we fight, which you already know. But the love? That just grows so much stronger. I have heard horror stories of wrong mates being matched by fate, but that is not the case for us."

I shuttered at the unexpected chill those words made shoot up my spine, "Yeah, I really hope those are just rumors."

Completely ignoring me, Kenya puckered up her lips for a kiss as Lizzie sashayed her way back to where we sat, "Reina, can you tell your friend over there to put those bright ass lips down? I am not getting that neon mess on me." Lizzie said as she plopped down in her chair. The three of us couldn't help but all laugh.

It felt good to be back home, though the more I recapped my honeymoon, the more I missed my mate. Since Lizzie was part of the royal guard, the waiter kept us topped off with only the top shelf mixtures. The alchemist had done a fabulous job of creating all types of alcoholic beverages mixed with blood that we could consume without getting sick, as long as we didn't go overboard with it. They held no nutritional value whatsoever, but they tasted good and being able to get tipsy was more than a little bit of fun. But, they did make us have to use the restroom, something we normally only did maybe twice a day. Me more so than others as evidenced by the squeaky chorus of, "Again?", I received from Lizzie and Kenya when I excused myself from the table.

The place wasn't jam packed but it did have a decent enough sized crowd that I had to say excuse me several times before I finally made my way to the restroom. There was less of a crowd there, sense most were still leery of the new drinks. Altogether the daunting task took probably less than two minutes.

I was headed back to where me and the girls had been seated when a rather large hand grabbed my upper arm and spun me around, "Josephine?", he said once we were face to face. His voice was deep and gravelly, and sent chills down my spine, and not in a good way.

"Uh, no. You've got the wrong girl." I said to him with a nervous laugh as I tried but failed to shrug him off, which should have been easy. He wasn't a vampire, or a shifter, so he wasn't stronger than me. I closed my eyes for a second to gain my composure and in that small amount of time I could sense that he was a warlock (and no, a warlock isn't just a male witch, but more like a war mage. And can be either a male or female), but something about him and his magic was just off. If felt crazed, erratic. "Dude, seriously, I'm not whoever you think I am."

"Josie, baby, it's me." Desperation laced his words and pulled at my heartstrings even though he truly gave me the heebie-jeebies. The silent tear that shed down from his eye that was swirling with magic strangely had sparks shooting up the birthmark on my hipbone.

"Hey, Rena. We got a problem here?" Bruno, one of the barrel-chested, brutal looking members of the royal guard came to the rescue just as the stranger was about to pull me closer to him. He grabbed the male's hand away from me while he said, "You just go 'head wit da girls and finish y'alls night whiles I have a word or two with our new friend here."

Right before I walked off I said to Bruno, "Don't be too hard on him, he just thought I was someone else." I almost changed my words when I looked down and saw a magic burn mark on my arm where he had been holding onto me.

"Are you okay?" Kenya asked once I made my way back to the table.

"Yeah, no, I don't know. That whole little encounter just felt...wrong. Maybe we should just go." As we parted ways I couldn't help the eerie feeling that I'd seen that mystery male before, and would again.

Chapter 2

I flashed myself into our bedroom without thinking. There were rose petals throughout the entire floor, along with candles on almost every surface; end tables, mantel, dresser. Once I began admiring it all was when I remembered Ricardo had asked me to *NOT* come in once I got home. I hurriedly flashed back out to our front walkway, but, it was quickly made apparent that I hadn't been fast enough.

"One thing woman, just one thing that I asked of you." Ricardo's disembodied voice came as a gentle whisper against the nape of my neck right before he materialized directly behind me. When he was fully corporeal, he swatted my behind with one hand while wrapping his arm around my waist. He then commenced with my mock chastisement, "Maybe I should spank you for being so naughty."

"Judging by that large bulge I feel that seems to be trying to rip its way out of your pants and into mine, you'd probably use any excuse you could to give me a spanking."

"Hmm...you could be quite right about that." Ricardo said with a touch of sensual laughter in his husky tone as he spun me around to face him. The Fates had truly been kind to me when they decided to pair me with such a male that was gorgeous on both the inside and out. He was about five inches taller than my five-foot six frame, so whenever we were face to face I was gazing upward into his shimmering golden eyes. Ricardo's face was the true definition of masculine beauty, the slight, black stubble on his jawline contrasted beautifully with his olive toned skin.

"Thank Nyx we have a long, long time to learn just how true that statement is."

"Baby, has anyone ever told you you talk too much?' I said to him as I reached up to grab the back up his head, those slick strands glided in between my fingers. But the simmering burn I began to feel along my skin once our lips met was not the one I had been anticipating.

Screams came from up and down the block as vampire children that had just been playing about cried out for their parents. Their tiny shrieks stopped almost as soon as they had begun, a sure sign their moms and dads hadn't waisted any time on rescuing their bundles of joy.

Steam wafted up from the ground as huge pellets of acid rain were dropping down from out of the sky, literally singeing our skin. Before I had the chance to do something stupid like open my mouth to speak, Ricardo grabbed me in a tight hold and flashed us both inside of the house. And not a moment too soon.

"What the fuck was that?" was the first thing that plopped out of my mouth once Ricardo set me on my feet in our living room. "Oh, honey, you even had dinner waiting." I whined once I noticed our regular donor, Olivia, who took one look at us and promptly fall straight to the floor. I would have too had the tables been reversed.

Skin was sloughing down from off of Ricardo's face, his once sculpted skin looked like a wax doll gone all wrong. I could feel my own skin sagging down and knew that even my eye sockets were exposed by the breeze I felt from the bottom of my eyeballs. It wouldn't take long for our skin to heal, but as we waited for that to happen we looked like two characters that just walked off a humans horror film set. One about zombies. Reminded me of the true decaying vampires, and neither of our bloodlines had any that I knew of. No, this was from the acid rain literally melting us.

Good thing we had already been given our emergency feeders, because this was one feeding Olivia wouldn't have survived. Feeders were the involuntary donors whom deserved death that the royal guard were assigned to pick up from earth; pedophiles, rapists, murderers, those who used other humans weaker than them.

After setting me down on my own two feet Ricardo flashed down to the cellar to grab our emergency donor. He made it back up right on time, I felt as though I was about to pass out right to the floor as my body pulled on everything it had to repair itself. My eyes felt like they had led weights on them, and I felt my body tipping over to the side. Right before I became up close and personal with the hardwood my fangs popped out in a knee jerk reaction as an already bleeding neck was shoved into my mouth.

After a few pulls of that delectable, regenerating blood, I consciously knelt down with the feeder still in my grips, and only hoped it wouldn't be too hard to get the few patches of skin that had fallen off of me out of the carpet beneath us. Once I truly felt the healing process start I looked over to see Ricardo feeding from the feeders wrist. After a few more deep pulls of the feeder's blood there was nothing more than a husk left in our arms.

In no mood to deal with a clean-up or much of anything else, I grabbed the empty husk as I got up and tossed it in the bin outside the back door while Ricardo just threw a blanket over poor Olivia. We then retired to our romantic looking room knowing the festivities planned would no longer take place.

"What the fuck was that out there?" I asked as I carefully peeled my dress away from my body, glad that I hadn't worn any pants, or underwear. "Acid rain? Seriously? We haven't seen anything like that since the wars were still going on."

Ricardo walked up behind me and lifted up the few strands of dress I must have missed. "No clue. Just must have been one pissed off wizard or witch in the neighborhood."

I turned around then motioned for him to do the same so that I could make sure all shreds of ruined clothing were also off of his body. "This is not the way I envisioned us stripping each other naked tonight." I said regretfully as I pealed away another strap of white from a back of sloughing muscles that resembled an old frail human male, "But for real, since the wars, most of the witches have been running around like they were recreating the human Woodstock. And having some sort of festival pretty much every month. They've been happy as jaybirds since Elyssia took her seat on the throne. And the wizards are for up close and personal, not random emotional outburst."

"Depending on how pissed they may have been, or maybe nuts." Ricardo said on a laugh as he turned back around so that we stood face to face, "But for as badly as the two of us look, makes me feel like that downpour had been aimed at us."

"When you say it like that." *What if it really had been aimed at us?* I thought to myself as those swirling eyes haunted me in my minds eye. I went on to tell him all about the encounter I had at the club, "You don't think he actually followed me home. Do you?"

Ricardo seemed just as troubled as I felt at that moment. He kept looking at different areas of my body trying to find a safe zone to grab onto me. He finally just grabbed both of my hands,

"Awe, *mi corazone*, the rain has stopped now. Even if it was this strange male you ran into, he is long gone now. Probably just had one too many of those new drinks." Ricardo continued as he pulled me towards the bed, "Come, let's just rest. Because when we rise, I plan on having the night I'd intended for us."

"Honey, I'd kiss you right now, grotesque looks and all, but I'm afraid both of our lips would literally fall off." We both laughed for a minute and gazed into the only part of our bodies that had already completely healed, our eyes. "I think snuggling should probably be taken off the table too."

We laid like that a few seconds longer before we let a deep healing sleep overtake us. Little did I know it would be one of the last peaceful sleeps I'd be having for a long time.

Chapter 3

"Well, at least you both are all healed up now. Too bad the same can't be said for poor Olivia. Poor thing had a damn mental breakdown. I actually picked her out personally for the two of you."

"Could I at least get the chance to open my eyes before you begin with the chastisement?" My body may have been healed, but it felt as though I were recovering from a battle with a pack of werewolves. There wasn't an area on my body that didn't feel raw. "It's bad enough that I'm starving and feel sick as shit all at the same time. And vampires aren't even supposed to be able to get sick."

"Well, after the acid bath you had, you're lucky you aren't re-growing any limbs."

At the very mention of loss limbs, I snatched off the covers to reassure myself everything was still intact. When I saw they were, I threw a pillow at my best-friends head, "Not funny, Anya!" she just laughed as she flashed from the door to the bed before the pillow even had a chance to touch her. "Get off of my bed, the only being I want checking me out is Ricardo."

She rolled her eyes at me while she laid back and said, "Yuck. Looking at you would be like looking at my sister. Besides, Kierra is all the female, and male that I need."

"Speaking of your mate, I haven't had a chance to see her yet either since we've been back. How is she and Lucas, and the rest of the highly screwed up royal vampire clan doing?" Anya's face scrunched up in response to that, which was completely out of character for her, "Come on, you know I'm just kidding. I practically grew up with the lot of you. Well, maybe not your sisters."

I quit talking when she looked at me like she was figuring out the most difficult question in all the realms, like the meaning of life or something. "Who's Lucas?"

"Are you high or something? What do you mean 'who's Lucas'?" when she continued to give me that same puzzled look I continued, "He's kind of hard to forget. Just as tall as Kierra, can sprout wings, has fangs, sometimes white, sometimes black. Oh! Here's one thing you def should remember! You pushed his big behind out same day Tia pushed out Jelissa." Still nothing, which gave me a really bad feeling. "You do remember Tia and Jelissa, don't you?"

That question earned me a shove along with a screeching, "Of course I remember who my sister and niece are!"

I shoved her royal must be high ass right back, "Well, seemed like a logical question to ask considering you can't remember your own damn son." I buried my head in my hands when all I got in response was that same vacant look again to muffle my scream before I said to her in a strained tone, "Dude, are friggin kidding me? You get defensive when I ask if you forgot your sister and niece, yet nothing at the mention of a son. Doesn't that seem off to you?"

It dawned on me then that there was a slightly messed up pattern going on. So I tried a little experiment, "Son," blank stare, "Lucas," Anya squinted her eyes like she was on the verge of a massive migraine. "Strip," I told Anya, then more to myself I said, "Leave for my honeymoon for just a few years and come back to a hot damn mess."

"Aren't you the one that was accusing me of taking a peak?" she asked while she started taking her clothes off. She knew I wouldn't have asked without a reason.

"I've got a feeling that little turd of yours must have done something really stupid, and I'm just hoping it was for a good reason. And there it is." As soon as she slid her shirt over her head I saw the rune I had been looking for, "That boy put a damn forget me knot rune dab smack in the middle of your back. And I'm more than sure everyone else has a matching one. And he must've spelled them so none of you could even see 'em. He couldn't get me since I wasn't here. And y'all wonder why I don't want any kids?"

"A rune? That's some angel crap isn't it?"

"Well, you did marry a half angel." I pointedly reminded her.

"Shit. Kierra!" she belted right before she pulled her shirt back over her head. As she hopped off of my bed she said, "Just when I thought I was coming over here to help with your drama looks like I need to head off and deal with my own. That acid rain was just the beginning, you've got some trouble headed your way, and you may need Elyssia more than me anyway."

"Full-blooded witches tend to not like my kind, Anya. You know that."

"Elyssia isn't just any full-blood, she's my sister, and their queen now. She'll treat you like family because you ARE my family, blood or not. She loves me and Tia regardless of our vampire side. When you get a chance to spend some real time with her, you'll know that too." When I went to protest she stopped me by saying, "Plus, you're going to have to finally embrace that other half of yourself to survive what's coming."

I rolled my eyes at that, "If it involves all that cryptic shit I'll pass."

"I know damned well she heard my loud ass mouth." Anya mumbled right before she bent down to give me a half hug and kiss on the cheek, "I'm only a call away, thanks to those phones Tia had the geeks give all of us when we went to find Jelissa. Yours and Ricardo's are over there on your dresser." She stood tall and said, "Wish me luck." Then flashed away.

Before she was completely gone I said, "When you find that boy kick his ass for me, then tell him I love him and give him a kiss."

"Should I be worried?" Ricardo asked as he flashed in with one eyebrow raised, not too long after Anya had left. "Anya said a hi, and bye, then grabbed Kierra and left."

"The reason I told you I don't mind waiting another hundred or so years before we even think about having any kids." Ricardo plopped down on the bed somewhere in the middle of me telling him the conversation I'd had with Anya. It was no wonder he had wanted to have our honeymoon far AWAY from Underlayes. We'd barely been home for a week and already drama was knocking at our door. "I have no clue what Lucas could be up to, but I do hope he's okay. Can you imagine how pissed all of them are gonna be once they figure out he made them forget him?"

"Awe, *la mia vita,*" Ricardo as he gathered me into his arms, "they will get the Lucas matter all sorted out. I'm sure he is more than fine. Far as this other thing Anya speaks of, we will worry about that when the time comes." He then allowed those magical hands of his to roam over my body, causing sensational chills everywhere he touched. "In the meantime, let's start practicing on how to make those babies we'll be having in a hundred years."

Chapter 4

"Now this right here is the one thing our honeymoon was missing." I said to Ricardo as a waiter handed us our *Bloody Mary's*, heavy on the blood. We were sitting in a couple of lounge chairs on the beach, not too far from the shore. Not that my mocha skin needed a tan or anything, but it sure felt good just being able to soak up the rays from the sun without the worry of going up in flames.

"*Mi amore*, if memory serves me well, you enjoyed the night life quite a bit." I could hear the sexy smirk in his tone without even a glance in his direction. "I lost count of how many humans you had, I was worried you'd succumb to blood lust."

I looked over at him then, knowing I'd see him slide those shades down the sexy, slender nose of his to give me a pointed look over them, and I was not disappointed. I couldn't help the school girl giggle that spilled from my lips at the sight of it, "I was not that bad." My giggle turned into an outright laugh when he cocked his head and stared at me that much harder. Matter of fact, I started laughing so hard I ended up with the hiccups.

With one eyebrow raised almost to his hairline, Ricardo said, "Maybe you should take it easy on that drink. It wasn't *that* funny."

I curtailed my laughter just enough to tell him I hadn't even drunk that much of it, right before I took a peak at said glass, "Whoa, guess I must've been thirsty."

"You know, just because you examine the cup, it will not make the drink reappear."

We stared at each other in mock seriousness for a moment, then both broke out laughing like a couple of teens. Next thing I knew I was straddling him on his lounge chair. Right as I was about to go in for a kiss the waiter was back with a refill for the both of us. As he sat them down on the small cocktail table, I asked him, "Is this one light on the liquor and heavy on the blood?" In response he just winked and walked away.

I went in for the kiss yet again until a couple of werepups began to howl at us and their parents cleared their throats rather loudly. Once they saw they had our attention they said, "This is a *family* beach in the daytime." I could tell they weren't angry by the twinkle in their eyes, but I could understand them not wanting the pups to see certain things.

With a, "My bad," I gave Ricardo a quick peck on the cheek as I climbed off and said to him, "Think I'll go shine my fangs before we go take a dip in the water."

The restroom wasn't too far from where we sat. For some reason it felt like it took forever to make it there. My legs felt like heavyweights had been attached to them, and my head was spinning like I'd had three times the amount of drinks I'd actually had. Right when I felt myself getting ready to trip over my own two feet, a set of strong hands gripped my upper arms from behind. Those large hands sent chills up and down my spine, and not in a good way.

All the thinned-out blood in my body went ice cold once I heard the voice that went along with said hands, "You really should be more careful." It was him, the crazed-out guy from the club. I couldn't have forgotten his voice had I tried.

I swallowed what little bit of spittle that was in my mouth as I did my best to regain my composure. Running into him again seemed like too much of a coincidence for me, and the creep factor went up about ten-thousand notches higher. Once I finally found my voice, it came a lot weaker than I'd liked, "As much as I appreciate you helping me to not fall flat on my face, I'd appreciate it even more if you moved your hands."

Before he did so I felt some type of surge go from his hands into body so strong that it went down to sear my very soul. It was like an electric shock that went straight through my bloodstream. My eyes clenched tight as visions began to flash behind my eyelids. Each image caused a searing pain to shoot through my brain like it was being placed there by a hot poker.

The images were flashbacks of a time long before Underlayes had even been created, of a life I had already lived and had no desire to go back to. There was a young couple that starred in them. Not surprisingly the male was the crazy that had just made the visions start appearing in the first place, and the female was a dead ringer for me, even down to the gestures she made and the dimple in her right cheek. Only difference was the brilliant icy blue color of her eyes that seemed even more vibrant with our mahogany skin tone.

For every ten or so happy flashes of the couple being so joyfully in love it was almost sickening, there was one that showed things weren't as perfect as they seemed. As the memories continued to fast forward along, she, I, wore the bruises and scars to prove it, both inside and out. But it wasn't the flashbacks that were causing the searing pain, it was the fact that the more they poured in, I felt my own present memories being snatched out.

"Snap out of it," my former self told me in a voice that seemed to bounce off the walls of my brain. She looked me with shear dread in her eyes as she cowed on the floor from yet another slap to the face, "we're stronger now. Don't let him turn us into this again. Fight!"

I pulled on that part of myself deep in the pit of my stomach that held a well of untapped magic that I had vowed I would never touch because of how much it frightened me, and just let go. I didn't know how to direct it, what to do with it, I just let instinct take complete control and absently hoped no one besides the monster in back of me would be hurt. The winds picked up causing the sand to shift this way and that, and every bird in the surrounding area to take flight as invisible waves and pulses of magic shot out of my body. Not only did it force my makeshift captor to lose the hold he had on me, both magical and physical, it made him fly across the beach to who knew where and also crumpled the entire restroom before me.

Once the magic was spent so was I. I collapsed on all fours with the entire world seeming as though it were spinning around me. I kept my eyes open long enough to see chaos all around me as families scrambled to gather one another and flee from the scene. As soon as I saw Ricardo speeding towards me, I stopped fighting it and promptly passed out.

Chapter 5

"As much as I love this extra attention and having you dote on me, we've got to start living a semi-normal life again." I said on a mock laugh to Ricardo.

It had been several weeks since the incident at the beach, but he was still afraid to let me out of his sight. Had the situation been the other way around I would have been the same way towards him. Every night since we'd flashed home that day I'd been wracked with dreams. Mostly more flashes from my previous life, some where I could feel *his* presence awaiting in the background. I would wake up in cold sweats, barely knowing my own identity. The best way to describe it? It was like being stuck in between a heavy fog and a nightmare I couldn't wake up from. The only thing I was absolutely sure of was the male that stood next to our bed with a fresh stack of pancakes, sausage links and a blood-orange smoothie on a tray that held a single rose in each corner. I took a deep inhale to let the aroma coat my nerves before I said what I had to say next.

"Why do I feel a major but coming along?" Ricardo wisely asked as he sat the tray in front of me and sat on the edge of the bed.

"Probably because of how wise you are." That earned me an eyebrow raised almost all the way to his hairline, "I may have a problem going back to work, since I don't remember anything about what I do."

Ricardo scrunched his eyes up at me and tilted his head to the side, "What on Underlayes are you talking about, *mi amore?*"

"This food looks so good, and I'm parched," I said to him as I downed my drink. I had thought I was ready; to come clean about the fact that I'd been keeping things from him. But when I really let it sink in that I had been pretty much lying to him, it felt like a betrayal, and I was afraid he'd see it as such. As I sat the glass back down on the tray I noticed that Ricardo hadn't moved an inch and was still staring me down, so I decided to just go ahead and spit it out, "I've been lying to you every morning that I've said everything's okay. I keep having dreams that aren't really dreams about my past life. And with every one of them, I lose a little bit more of myself. I'm losing my own memories. It's like whatever he did to me that day is still affecting me. If I don't do something about it soon, I'm pretty sure I'm going to be lost."

I gave Ricardo a minute or two for all of that to sink in. I watched as his eyes went to red then back to black again, though a twitch remained in his left eye I continued, "I have a plan though. And yes, you were right, there is a huge but coming. So, here it is." Ricardo snarled just a bit when I cleared my throat, "But, you're not going to like it."

"Before you continue on and tell me this hairbrained scheme of yours that I'm more than positive you've cooked up with Anya, Elyssia, and Kenya, right?" He ended that statement like it was a question. Even though I knew he knew the answer, I nodded my head in confirmation. "Let me see if I can get this straight." Ricardo got up from the bed then and began to pace to the door and back again. Which was kind of sexy as hell since all he was wearing was a pair of black jogging pants. "All of those days you woke up in a cold sweat and claimed you must have fed from a diabetic, you were lying?" He paused again, waiting on a response from me. After another head nod he went back to my deserved interrogation, "The mornings you shot up in the bed screaming and said you'd had a nightmare about losing your fangs, another lie. When you attributed forgetting about important dates like Kenya's birthday to a donor having been on drugs, just more lies." Finally, he stopped pacing and looked directly at me with his face as tight as I'd ever seen it, and said in a tone so cold it sent chills down my spine, "I'm your mate. How can I possibly protect you if I haven't a clue what I'm protecting you from? How could you look me in the eye and lie to me day after day?" He deadlocked onto my eyes when he said the next, "Why Reina? Oh, I know what you're going to say, but I want to hear it from your lips."

"Say what?" Ricardo's fangs shot down from his gums at that, so I decided playing dumb wasn't the right route to go. "I didn't want to worry you." He scoffed at that. "I was afraid of how you'd react. I wanted to at least come up with some type of plan first before I let you know..."

I didn't even get a chance to finish that train of thought since I was then talking to deaf ears. Ricardo had started laughing, and not a normal laugh either. It was one of those laughs that people do when they can no longer hold their shit together. He had thrown his head back and was cackling like a crazed maniac. I thought it best to just say nothing at all until he had gained at least a little bit of his composure.

Once the laughter died down, he crossed his arms over his chest and said to me in a voice that was still full of sinister, maniacal laughter, "Afraid of how I'd react? As if I'm the same type of monster your mate was in that former life?"

"That's not what I-"

"Not what you meant?" He shouted as he walked towards me. He stopped mid-step when noticed me involuntarily scooch back away from him. Ricardo rubbed at his temples, "Wow. I need out of here for a bit. Anya did say we have full access to the donors whenever we felt the need, yes?" I nodded at that, then he flashed away without another word.

***

"What did you do to your male to cause him to go through just about every involuntary donor we have?"

"Dammit Anya! One day I'm going to rearrange all of the furniture just to see you land on your ass!" I had still been staring at the spot Ricardo had flashed from when Anya decided to flash herself not only in my bedroom, but right into the bed next to me. Goddess only knew how long I had been staring at that same spot, willing him to be back in it. The beautiful breakfast he'd made me sat untouched in front of me, and looked like a soggy pile of crap. "What's the purpose of giving us those gadgets if you're not even going to use them yourself?"

"What can I say? I'm an old-fashioned type of girl. I'd rather just pop on in instead of calling or texting. Plus, if you move the furniture, I'd *see* it anyway." Anya reached down into a pocket of uncharacteristic jeans and pulled out a vial of blood. She handed it to me, "Take this. I don't have much time, got a kid to go wrangle up from Detroit. Did I tell you he has a friggin ice cream truck? Never mind, you probably forgot. Anyway, drink this."

"What is it?"

"It's something Elyssia cooked up with some of Kierra's blood for extra potency. It should stop you from losing any more memories until everything else is all said and done. I'm assuming the reason we have to restock the cells with more human low lives to feed from is that you already told Ricardo about the plan?" She asked as she stole a chocolate covered strawberry off my plate.

"Nope. I was getting ready to. But after I admitted to all the lies, the conversation was put on hold." I heard Anya take a breath like she was about to say something and stopped her before she could, "Don't you dare say I told you so. Yes, you were right, lying to your mate is always a bad idea. Yada, yada, yada." Then I looked at her and blew her a raspberry.

"Gross!" She shouted at me.

"Well, serves you right for flashing your ass into my bed, jerkwad."

Anya just laughed as she reached across me and grabbed a napkin to wipe her arm off, "Don't get mad at me just because I was right, and you were bullheaded." She slightly sobered up from her laughter before she continued, "Anyway, back to the other reason I popped over here. Lizzie and Kenya have finished up the arrangements. Ironically, you'll be in Detroit. Where for whatever reason we always end up at in these types of situations."

"That isn't really that weird. The closest portal does go to Detroit."

"Guess you're right. Whatever. You won't know where the hell you are anyway. The spot they chose for you is pretty much secluded, which is why they picked it. Maybe afterwards it can be a vacation spot or something."

Anya pulled a set of keys from her pocket. I thought she was about to hand them to me, but instead she threw them across the room where a very bloody Ricardo flashed in just in time to grab them. Before he could say a word she told him, "I'll let your lady love here explain what those are for." Then she grabbed me in a tight hug and whispered in my ear, even though I'm sure Ricardo still heard her, "I won't be around for the main events, the beginning of which has been moved up to tonight, but you got this. You're more witch than vamp, just like Tia, and that's not always a bad thing. Love you."

"Love you too." I said to her as she pulled back.

"K. I'm off to go beat a son that made me forget about him, literally." The next was directed at Ricardo, "Yes, she fucked up, but she was scared and did it out of love. Take care of my girl." Then she was gone. And I was left alone to face the music.

Ricardo looked as if he were about to speak. Before he had a chance to, I threw myself into his bloody arms. "I'm so sorry," I said to him, "I never meant to lie to you. But admitting what was going on out loud made it all just too real. And what we're going to have to do next sucks enough as it is."

At first Ricardo remained as stiff as a board. Then he finally loosened up a bit and wrapped his arms around me, "Never keep me in the dark like that again."

"Ironically, you're the one that's about to put me in the dark."

***

"Can't I at least keep my bra on? I didn't get the perky vampire tits, mine fall off to the side like a couple of bean bags."

Little did I know Anya wasn't overexaggerating. Turned out the reason she had been in such a hurry was that the ritual part of the plan was taking place that night. Once I had finished telling the plan to Ricardo, Kenya, Lizzie and Elyssia, Anya's younger sister that was full witch, were at our front door.

The plan? We'd had Kenya and Lizzie over a night after the incident at the beach. Kenya had 'felt' another presence inside of me. After further investigation, yes, behind Ricardo's back, she'd come to realize Jonathan, the whack job that started this mess, had implanted a back door inside of my mind. The flashes or memory that I had been having was him working to revert my current soul back to it's former self; something that neither the present or old me wanted. Which was why with every dream I had, a little bit more of me was lost. My soul literally needed to be cleansed.

My soul would be extracted from my body, leaving just enough of so that I would still be me, and still be mated to Ricardo. But, there wouldn't be enough where I would have any memories at all. I'd be like one of those human amnesia victims. Only until my soul was cleaned up and returned to my body; which could take anywhere from six weeks to six years. However long it took didn't matter, I couldn't take the risk of losing myself. Wouldn't risk losing all the memories of those that I loved, the goals I'd worked so hard to accomplish. I was a violinist, and already the terms bravado and forte meant nothing to me. Not for some warlock that couldn't let go of the past. Fuck that. And I wasn't about to take a chance of the bond I had with the male that stood at my side being broken.

"Rena, will you please stop fidgeting?" Kenya asked me, again.

"You aren't the one laying but ass naked on a cold slab, now are you?" I complained. Ricardo gave my hand a reassuring squeeze. He knew as well as they did the real reason I couldn't stay still was because of how nervous I was.

Elyssia had not only made a circle on the ground enclosing the four of us inside, she also put the entire backyard in a dome of water. It was like being on the inside of a snow globe, minus the snow. No one could see inside of it, or even sense that any of us were there. To any passerby it would appear as if everyone was gone, just in case Jonathan sensed his spell being meddled with. With everything in place Jonathan wouldn't realize anything until we were long gone.

"Let's get this show on the road while the spell is still good and strong." Elyssia said to us with her arms raised. Her hair floated in the air while her eyed seemed like to pools of water. The fact that she wasn't quoting any movie lines at us let us know that we needed to hurry up. And that I needed to keep still and shut up.

"Okay, I'm good. I'll see all of you on the other side." I closed my eyes and waited. Minus any more complaints.

At first all I felt was a gentle pull from Kenya stood by the top of my head right where my soul chakra was. Then all of a sudden it became a full-on burn like she was taking a serrated edge machete to pry my head open with. I wanted to scream, to vomit, to fight, to do whatever it took to get away from the pain. Kenya or Elyssia must have put some sort of paralyzing spell on me because there was nothing that I could do besides just lay there and take it.

As terrified as I was to just let go, knowing that I would be nothing more than a shell of myself after I woke up, I finally gave in and fell into the deep oblivion that awaited me. All I could do was hope and pray to both Sekhmet and Nyx that my friends didn't fuck this up.

Chapter 6

I don't know why so many people always wish they had a do over in life. I mean, I guess I get it in a way. And probably more-so would if what happened to me hadn't happened. But it did.

I had no memory of the life I led before being turned. Ricardo, my Fated One, and I had been together for only a year, but it felt like I knew him for much longer than that. He said that memory loss was something that sometimes happened to the newly turned. I took his word for it, since that's not exactly something you can just look up on Google without finding a bunch of nonsense. And we stayed in a pretty tight-lipped community, amongst others like us. But no one delved into anyone else's business. There were some we were friendly with, but not really friends. He said the night he turned me I had been on the brink of death, that he had found me in an alley left for dead. That he knew me before in passing and couldn't just let me die. We've been together ever since. Even though the story sounded like a crock of shit to me, I trusted him enough to let it ride.

The mansion we lived in was almost as large as a castle, he said it had been in his family for hundreds of years. It was in a secluded location and kept mainly to ourselves, rarely did we go anywhere other than our own backyard. Not that I was complaining or anything, it would just be nice to have some type of interaction with others that didn't act like they had a five-yard stick stuck up they ass.

I had just woken up after having yet another dream that felt like much more than just that, with my entire body feeling as if I had just done an entire triathalon the night before. I sat up and put my head in my hands, my head felt like it was in a vice grip from hell. It had been happening for the past few weeks and had been getting worse instead of better.

I climbed out of bed, careful to not wake Ricardo. It was early still, but I had no intentions of going back to sleep, no way was I risking having another one of those dreams. They hurt too much to wake up from. They weren't nightmares, far from it, but when I woke up they were fragments I couldn't manage to piece together. But for some reason I almost always found myself if not in pain, then in tears when I woke up from them. And not just that, there was some form of power inside of me trying to break free, but I had no idea what it was or how to access it, yet.

Stepping into the bathroom I didn't bother with turning on the light, just slipped my black lace chemise over my head and stepped into our large, walk-in shower, and turned the water as hot as I could bare it. As I stood there directly under the spray flashes of a man kept appearing behind my eyelids. I could barely make out his features, but for whatever reason not being able to recognize him made me more than just sad, but hollow inside like something was missing.

"Rena, why are you up so early love? The sun has just barely set." As quiet as I had been getting out of the bed, I must have still woken Ricardo. I was so lost in thought that I hadn't even heard him open the shower door. He stood directly behind me and pulled my body flush against his own, swept my hair to the side and gently grazed his fangs along the crook of my neck before letting them sink into my skin.

Ricardo was not a male of many words, but what he lacked in syllables he made up for in sensation. His cold body grew warmer as he fed from me, I could feel his shaft growing and hardening against the crease of my ass. The water cascaded down both of our bodies as he licked the bite marks closed, and his large hands began to work their magic. With one hand, he began kneading my breast, squeezing right to the borderline between pleasure and pain as his other slid down to my hips then around my waist until it found the shaved, heated entrance that was waiting for him. He slipped his fingers, not inside of me, but only slid them along my tight, wet folds, then to tweak and tug at my clitoris, the sensation of that alone enough to put me on the verge of climax.

I whimpered as he removed his hand, but he was by no means done with me yet. Ricardo bent me slightly, splaying his pale ivory hand over my own, much smaller mocha one, interlacing our fingers along the tiles of the shower as I grabbed onto it for purchase. He then entered me in one swift, hard stroke. I screamed out as the feel of his long, wide shaft filled me so completely that if he wasn't an expert at using it, it would have hurt, instead it felt so good that my juices were already flowing around him. I came again as he found that perfect rhythm, his heavy length sliding up against my walls, the sensation making me so dizzy I would have lost my grip on the wall had he not still had hold of my hand. The water from the showerhead only added to the sensations.

Just as I felt myself coming to a full-on climax, the lightning bolt shaped mark on my outer thigh began to burn. The pain of it made me bend over further, making him not only go deeper, but also tighten even further around him. I became a mixture of both pleasure and true pain all at once, I could barely recognize which of the two my moans reflected. Ricardo slid out of me then, and before I had a chance to feel the emptiness of his shaft no longer there, he had me turned around, lifted up with a crushing grip on my hips, and was impaling me once again. As though he felt a sense of urgency, he pistoned in and out of me even harder and faster than before, which took my mind away from the flaring pain in my thigh.

As Ricardo gave me another stroke so deep inside of me I felt his sac rubbing against my entrance I screamed out with one last climax as he jettisoned inside, the warm trickling feel of it making me come that much harder. But when I closed my eyes, I was looking into the metallic silver irises that haunted my dreams, and they looked angry as hell. I could almost hear a faint, foreign, yet familiar voice in the back of my mind saying, *I will find you.*

When I opened my eyes, Ricardo was staring straight into mine, but it felt like he was seeing right through me to somewhere else, especially when he said, "She's mine."

Before I could ask him anything or think any further, he claimed my lips in a claiming, almost punishing kiss. Then I felt a tiny pinprick on the side of my hip and promptly blacked out.

***

Halfway across the world from where Ricardo and Rena were, a warlock wearing only a pair of black shorts knelt down on the ground in the rain in the dark of night in a cemetery, the droplets shimmered down his muscled, ebony chest and back. He summoned the lightning to the palms of his outstretched hands, letting it empower him further, as he called out to his ancestors. "Ancestors, my foremothers, and forefathers, I come to you tonight, the anniversary of the night you gifted me with one of my greatest gifts, to ask your help in finding her. Help me bring her back to where she belongs, at my side."

The storm became malevolent then, lightning struck around Jonathan left and right, which both fueled and empowered him. He threw his head back as he soaked it all in. As he closed his eyes, his haunches rose when he finally saw her, with the vampire that had somehow ensnared his powerful, beautiful mate. He tried yet again to communicate with her through their mark, but something was blocking him still, but he felt it slipping, and that little slip was all he needed to learn her location.

Reaching into his back pocket, Jonathan pulled out his phone and dialed his brother. Without bothering with any pleasantries, all he said was, "It's time to hunt us down a vampire, and bring home my mate."

Chapter 7

When I woke back up maybe an hour or two later, I heard voices coming from downstairs. I would have just flashed down there to see what was going on, but I felt too shaky. Besides, as low as they were talking, I'm pretty sure I wasn't meant to hear whatever was being said. So instead of either flashing or walking down the decadent spiral staircase, I crept over to the bedroom door instead and opened it just a crack. Good thing the hinges were well oiled. Hell, for it to be such an old home it was very well maintained on the inside; practically everything seemed brand new.

"...breaking through the wards already?" Ricardo was asking someone, and he didn't sound too happy either.

"Probably because none of us realized just how powerful he is." a female seethed right back at in reply. "He shouldn't have been able to get past the injections the alchemists cooked up for you to give to her."

"Y'all shoulda just listened to me in the first place and just killed his ass." Yet another disembodied voice chimed in, it was such a husky tone I couldn't make out whether it belonged to male or female.

From the sound I heard and the comment Ricardo made after I'm pretty sure they must have fist bumped one another, "Now that is a plan I'm completely on board with."

The amount of "ughs" that followed that comment made me wonder just how many people were down there. Since it was night and the lights were on I was pretty sure they weren't all vampires. But I didn't recognize any of the voices.

"You knumbskulls!" the first female whisper-shouted, "We couldn't risk killing him before her soul had been cleansed. She needs to have at least a fighting chance with how strong of a connection he made with her. Killing him could have very we killed her. We have no way of knowing for certain one way or the other. Don't you think I'd like to feel the fuckers blood running through my fingers too?"

"And now?"

"They're almost done, but, we haven't found a way to completely disenchant his spell yet." She paused for a moment before she continued, "Time, once again, isn't on our side."

"Is there anything that *is* on our side?" Ricardo's voice grew more intense with each question he asked. He was barely bothering to whisper anymore. "We shouldn't have stayed so close to Underlayes."

"Wouldn't have mattered where you went," another female spoke up, she sounded like she was fresh off the boat from Africa, "that crazy male would still have found where she was eventually. And the hairbrained scheme you had of telling nothing of the truth, I still cannot believe you did that. How will she protect herself from what she does not know? Hmm, genius? Were you drinking from a cracked out human when you thought that one up?"

"I can protect her."

"Males." She seethed right back at him. "You make me so glad I am gay. What magic do you have to protect her with on your own? Brute strength and fangs is not always the answer. At least if she knew the truth maybe she could have accessed her own by now."

I really didn't like the direction the conversation was going, it sounded they were talking about a really messed up movie. The more I listened the more I was convinced they had to have been talking about me. As much as every instinct within me demanded I confront them all about what was going on, I wanted to hear more first. I was sure they wouldn't be so loose lipped if I stood front and center during their convo.

Whether they'd planned on saying more or not about what I was apparently being kept in the dark about was beyond me. Right at that moment the entire mansion shook like an earthquake had just hit. I couldn't decipher who was saying what after that from the ringing that started in my ears.

"He's here, and I'm thinking he brought friends."

"Why are they even working with him?"

"They don't know the truth. Turns out he never told them he killed his mate. He just told them she was missing."

I went down to my knees as the ringing became a piercing shrill trying to embed itself into my brain. I slapped both of my hands on the sides of my head, self-consciously hoping that somehow would stop debilitating noise. It didn't.

I could just barely make out the shouts and sounds of flesh pounding against flesh, along with the echoes of furniture and glass being broken downstairs. I most definitely could smell the blood that was being spilt. The sweet aroma of it had me vamping out even in the midst of all of that agony. My fangs elongated and my facial features began to transform.

It wasn't until I was down on all fours down on all fours with my palms planted firmly on the floor that I realized a few things; this master bedroom truly was huge, we didn't have much furniture in it, having white carpet in it was a dumb ass idea, and I wasn't alone.

There were three pairs of feet in front of me. Whether they were male or female I couldn't tell since they all had on steel toed combat boots along with some type of dark purple ceremonial robes. Next thing I knew I had ended up in the middle of the floor somehow, I could faintly hear them chanting and figured the excruciating pain in my head came from them. As difficult as it was, I lifted my head to bare my fangs and hiss at them. Upon actual visualization I saw that there was more than three of them, their faces cloaked by the hoods they wore. They surrounded me in a circle with their hands clasped together, probably drawing power from each other.

I also noticed they were getting closer to me, and something told me that if they touched me, I'd be the one to regret it. Going on nothing more than pure instinct I brought my hands up then slammed them back down onto the floor. From some well deep inside of me that I didn't even know existed magic shot out of me, not just my palms but from my entire body. The shockwaves of it knocked them all down and more importantly, away from me. With them incapacitated the ringing and pain in my head disappeared as though it had never been there.

What I did next shocked the hell out of me. As two of them began to pick themselves up from off the floor on either side of me. I outstretched my arms and when they rose I made a motion in the air like I was raking them down with my claws from their necks to the bottom of their torso. They dropped right back down to the floor. And even though I made no physical purchase, their blood and flesh were rendered beneath my claws. There may have been too many of them for me to take completely down on my own, but I damn sure wasn't going down without a fight.

I pounced on another of my assailants that was directly in front of me that made a fatal attempt to stand. I was on top of her in less than a split second and buried my fangs in her throat, after a few pulls to refuel I ripped it out and watched as it pooled into the plush, white carpet.

I was headed towards my next victim when someone shouted an immobilizing, "Stop!" from behind me. Not a single limb would budge. The only part of my body I had control over was my eyes.

My body began to lift to a standing position, and not because I was commanding it. Out of the corner of my eye I saw a tall, handsome, ebony toned male walk around until he stood in front of me. Finally, I stopped rising once I was a little over a foot from the floor.

Once we were finally face to face he spoke in a deeply shocked yet disappointed tone to his comrades while staring me dead in the eye, "This isn't her. Dear Gods. She may indeed be either a doppelgänger or reincarnation, but this is not my mother. Josephine was a lot of things, but she wasn't a vampire." If it hadn't been for the fact that he and his cronies were trying to either kill or kidnap me, or whatever else, I would've felt sorry for him as a single tear shed from his left eye. His voice gave an almost imperceptible crack when he said, "My father truly has lost his mind. It's time to admit he must've killed her."

There were tons of moans and groans as the rest of his motley crew came to and they all started to speak at once.

"What is he saying?"

"How can he be sure?"

"Knew this was total bullshit."

Mister Tall Dark and Handsome directed his next words to me, "I'm sorry for all of this. The warlocks you just killed, that's on me and my family, not you. I'm going to let you go, but don't waste your time trying to fight us anymore. You need to get out there and save your mate. My dad wants to try and break your bond, by killing him."

Once he let me go and didn't bother to utter damn word. All I cared about was finding Ricardo before it was too late.

Chapter 8

It wasn't until I flashed my not so happy or lucky ass outside that I remembered I had on nothing but that damn black chemise. Oh, well. Winter or not, at least I didn't have to worry about catching frostbite.

For whatever dumb reason I flashed to the front yard, even though common sense said the backyard. But, given the fact that most of our backyard was pool and furniture. So of course, that's exactly where I heard the commotion coming from.

My adrenaline was running far too high for me to risk flashing again, so I used my vampire speed to get to the backyard instead. And I didn't make it back there a moment too soon.

In all the movies when something drastic is about to happen it goes to slow motion. Well, I can't really say if things sped up or slowed down, time just didn't even exist to me. All that existed right then and there was the warlock that looked like he'd just escaped the insane asylum standing over a beaten and bloody Ricardo with a big ass sword, ready to take his head off. Literally.

I didn't waste a second to stop and analyze the situation, I couldn't. I ran headfast to where the two of them were along the edge of the pool. Once again I allowed pure instinct to drive me. I made there in between the two of them just before the sword made purchase and lifted my arm to block; sort like what Anna did in Frozen to save her sister. Only instead of turning into a block of ice I had my arm sliced off right below my elbow, which gave Ricardo just enough time to roll out the way.

Ricardo made a move as if to stand, "Lay your ass right there." I scolded him, "This is my fight."

Then I shocked myself, and everyone else looking when I manifested a sword of my own and blocked El' Cookoo when he tried to go for yet another killing blow on Ricardo. It was on from there. We fought with pure strength and skill, a skill I didn't even know I possessed. I could see in his swirling irises that he was extremely powerful, but that power was unchecked and useless because his mind was no longer intact. I could see the love he carried for his long gone mate, and I could also see his guilt that confirmed he was the one who had killed her. I could just about see into his very soul as we parried with one another, going strike for strike, neither of us landing a killing blow.

But I had the advantage over him. Warlocks needed to breathe, vampires didn't. As close as we were to the pool, I made a spinning move that made us both go in and under. His steel toe boots took him straight to the bottom and I followed right behind him. He got in a few good strikes after that, but I just smiled as I watched him struggle for air. Then I just laughed under the water and looked him straight in the eyes as I sliced his head clean off his body.

When I swam back to the surface there were a variety of beings making their way out of the back sliding doors; all of them bloody, some of them limping, one of them with wings.

I threw down my sword as Ricardo limp-raced over to where I climbed out of the pool. I let him gather me into his arms and kiss me as though his life depended on it. Once the kiss ended I took a step back and slapped the shit out of him, "Plan on telling me what the fuck is going on?"

***

Three months later...

I was in our true backyard back in Underlayes playing the Concerto on my violin, with my regrown limb. Something I feared I'd never do again. The chalky rosin from my bow giving off a slight film in the air, the bravado from my wrist and finger-tips rocking shaking the strings, giving it that perfect sound. Just the thought of going the rest of my existence without it was just too much to bare.

After everything had been said and done in Detroit, and the truth of it all had been explained to clueless me, we went back through the portal. After burning down the mansion with all the dead bodies in it. They told me the risks of having my soul placed back in my body without it being fully cleansed, especially with Jonathan being dead by my hand. But I couldn't wait any longer. Not after all that had transpired in that short amount of time.

Luckily it had been cleansed just enough to where all of my memories were back and intact, with only a few of the former ones left. Along with the memory of her being killed by her own mate during a fit of rage. Knowing his family were just as much of his victims as both I and Josephine were, I went to them to tell them the when and how of it. They deserved to have the closure he had denied them.

All in all, everything worked out for the best. And we lived Happily Ever After, until the next crisis anyway.

The End

Don't miss out!

Visit the website below and you can sign up to receive emails whenever T. A. Moorman publishes a new book. There's no charge and no obligation.

https://books2read.com/r/B-A-WEBG-MWCFB

BOOKS 2 READ

Connecting independent readers to independent writers.

Did you love *In My Dreams*? Then you should read *Chocolate Vanilla Swirl*[1] by T. A. Moorman!

Bound and determined to spread his wings and live his life to its fullest, nowhere near his parents, Lucas decides to take a trip to the human realm. Especially since he has a mate that refuses to settle down with him, be with him physically in any way, or even admit to it out loud that they belong together. So, he figures the best thing for them to do is to stay as far away from each other as possible. Even if that means leaving Underlayes, and everyone else he loves behind. But when he gets his first taste of life, and ice cream, he may not be in such a big hurry to get back home.

1. https://books2read.com/u/bP0M17

2. https://books2read.com/u/bP0M17

What Lucas doesn't realize is that his parents kept him secluded from the world for a reason. Anya, his mother, is an elemental witch/vampire. Kierra, his father, half angel, half gender shifting demon. Which makes him...

When the angels from Heaven and the hounds of Hell sense his presence Lucas may just get a lot more than he bargained for. Especially with him being part vampire and witch, heaven and hell aren't the only ones that could take claim. The question is will the other dieties step in to help, or agree that he shouldn't even exist?

This can be read as a standalone. But may be a lot more fun when read in order.

Including a bonus Underlayes Short Story

Read more at gothicmoms.blogspot.com.

Also by T. A. Moorman

About the Author

When you become a Mom, you begin to put yourself last, and your combat boots begin to collect dust. Going to your child's PTA meetings in full Gothic, especially industrial, regalia is pretty much frowned upon. Especially by your own children, and your teens would die of a heart attack. But, one should not have to completely stop being themselves, uniqueness is greatness. So all of that darkness is put into words in her books, and designs in her jewelry sold in her Gothic Moms Dark Charms shop on Etsy and Rebels Market.

Single mother of five beautiful children, but by far more than just that. T. A. Moorman is an artist, a former violinist, a seamstress, a crafter, a writer, a blogger, a reviewer, a dark confidant and a darkly dangerous, fiercely protective friend. She still hopes to one day find her Dark Knight in shining armor, since

Prince Charming would never be able to handle her. And currently broke, so go buy something of hers. Lol.

Read more at gothicmoms.blogspot.com.

www.ingramcontent.com/pod-product-compliance
Lightning Source LLC
Chambersburg PA
CBHW030829060726
47590CB00004B/1454